Samuel French Acting Edition

Off Off Broadway Festival Plays 42nd Series

Breakfast Scene
by Eric Marlin

Jack + Jill
Book & Lyrics by Sarah Hammond
Music by Emily Goldman

Sir
by Jahna Ferron-Smith

Square Footage
by Jessica Moss

this movie
by Amanda Keating

What Happened at the Dolphin Show
by Miranda Rose Hall

SAMUELFRENCH.COM   **SAMUELFRENCH.CO.UK**

FOR PRODUCTION ENQUIRIES

UNITED STATES AND CANADA
Info@SamuelFrench.com
1-866-598-8449

UNITED KINGDOM AND EUROPE
Plays@SamuelFrench.co.uk
020-7255-4302

Each title is subject to availability from Samuel French, depending upon country of performance. Please be aware that *OFF OFF BROADWAY FESTIVAL PLAYS 42ND SERIES* may not be licensed by Samuel French in your territory. Professional and amateur producers should contact the nearest Samuel French office or licensing partner to verify availability.

No one shall make any changes in this title(s) for the purpose of production. No part of this book may be reproduced, stored in a retrieval system, or transmitted in any form, by any means, now known or yet to be invented, including mechanical, electronic, photocopying, recording, videotaping, or otherwise, without the prior written permission of the publisher. No one shall upload this title(s), or part of this title(s), to any social media websites.

For all enquiries regarding motion picture, television, and other media rights, please contact Samuel French.

MUSIC USE NOTE

Licensees are solely responsible for obtaining formal written permission from copyright owners to use copyrighted music in the performance of this play and are strongly cautioned to do so. If no such permission is obtained by the licensee, then the licensee must use only original music that the licensee owns and controls. Licensees are solely responsible and liable for all music clearances and shall indemnify the copyright owners of the play(s) and their licensing agent, Samuel French, against any costs, expenses, losses and liabilities arising from the use of music by licensees. Please contact the appropriate music licensing authority in your territory for the rights to any incidental music.

IMPORTANT BILLING AND CREDIT REQUIREMENTS

If you have obtained performance rights to this title, please refer to your licensing agreement for important billing and credit requirements.

The Samuel French Off Off Broadway Short Play Festival (OOB) has been the nation's leading short play festival for forty-two years. The OOB has served as a doorway to future success for aspiring writers. Over 200 plays have been published, and many participants have become established, award-winning playwrights.

For more information on the Samuel French Off Off Broadway Short Play Festival, including history, interviews, and more, please visit www.oobfestival.com.

Festival Artistic Director: Casey McLain
Literary Coordinator: Garrett Anderson
Editorial Coordinator: Sarah Weber
Production Coordinators: Caitlin Bartow, Coryn Carson, Carly Erickson
Marketing Team: Chris Kam, Courtney Kochuba, Ryan Pointer
Festival Publicity Director: Abbie Van Nostrand
Stage Manager: Laura Manos-Hey
House Manager: Tyler Mullen
Box Office Manager: Rosemary Bucher
Announcer: Coryn Carson
Festival Staff: Jennifer Carter, Charles Graytok, Kate Karczewski, David Kimple, Nicole Matte, Ryan McLeod, Elizabeth Minski, Kevin Peterson, Theresa Posorske, Jonah Rosen, Becca Schlossberg, Alejandra Venancio
Festival Interns: Ella Andrew, Sasha Bartol, Tommy Heller, Rebecca Roberts, Rachel Smith

HONORARY GUEST PLAYWRIGHT
Will Eno

FESTIVAL JUDGES
Rachel Bonds
John Clinton Eisner
James Hindman
Ciera Iveson
Abigail Katz
Andrew Leynse
Emily Morse
Jiehae Park
Jonathan Silverstein
Michael Walkup
Susan Westfall
Lauren Yee

TABLE OF CONTENTS

FOREWORD

Samuel French is honored to have the seven daring and inspirational playwrights included in this collection as the winners of our 42nd Annual Off Off Broadway Short Play Festival. This year our Festival received over 1,000 submissions from around the world. We thank all of these gifted playwrights for sharing their talent with us and welcome each writer into our elite group of Off Off Broadway Festival winners.

We also wish to thank the producing companies who helped stage these works at our Festival. The vital relationship between playwright and theatre is one that we know well at Samuel French. Whether producing a Tony-winning play or developing a new work, theatre companies play a vital role in cultivating new audiences and communicating a playwright's vision. We commend them for this mission and thank each of the producers involved in the 42nd Annual Festival for their tireless dedication and contributions to their playwright.

Perhaps the most challenging part of the OOB Festival is our production week. From our initial pool of Top Thirty playwrights, we ultimately select six plays for publication and representation by Samuel French. Of course, we can't make our selection alone, so we enlist some brilliant minds within the theatre industry to help us in this process. Each night of the Festival, we have an esteemed group of three judges consisting of a Samuel French playwright and two other members of the theatre industry. We thank them for their support, insight, and commitment to the art of playwriting.

Samuel French is a 188-year-old company rich in history while at the same time dedicated to the future. We are constantly striving to develop groundbreaking methods which will better connect playwright and producer. With a team committed to continuing our tradition of publishing and licensing the best new theatrical works, we are boldly embracing our role in this industry as bridge between playwright and theatre.

On behalf of our board of directors; the entire Samuel French team in our New York, Los Angeles, and London offices; and the over 10,000 playwrights, composers, and lyricists that we publish and represent, we present you with the six winning plays of the 42nd Annual Samuel French Off Off Broadway Short Play Festival.

Get ready to be inspired.

Casey McLain
Artistic Director
The Samuel French Off Off Broadway Short Play Festival

Breakfast Scene

Eric Marlin

BREAKFAST SCENE was produced as part of the Samuel French Off Off Broadway Short Play Festival at the Classic Stage Company in New York City on August 8, 2017. The production was directed by Ilana Khanin. The cast was as follows:

GEORGETTE MAGRITTE...............................Annie Hoeg

RENÉ MAGRITTE ....Ry Szelong

COWBOY .... Ben Dawson

CHARACTERS

GEORGETTE MAGRITTE – female, mid-twenties to mid-forties, any race

RENÉ MAGRITTE – male, but can be played by a woman, around the same age as the actor playing Georgette, any race

COWBOY – male, mid-twenties to mid-thirties, any race

SETTING

the Magrittes' kitchen in the early morning

AUTHOR'S NOTES

the actors playing the Magrittes do not need to look like the real Magrittes

a multiplicity of identities onstage is the preference including, but not limited to, race, gender, body type, and physical ability, with all roles open to trans and gender non-conforming performers

the masturbation sequence should be done extremely privately
and extremely quietly
with zero titillation
luridness
or shock
there are no clichéd orgasmic moans
it is not pornographic
it should not "look like masturbation"
it is not performed for our benefit
it is not performed at all
it is not meant for the audience
it is a personal, matter-of-fact, autonomous moment

the silences aren't heavy
they just are

in general, the less flourish there is to the delivery of the language, the better

nobody cries

(Typical morning.)

*(***RENÉ*** and ***GEORGETTE MAGRITTE*** waiting for coffee to brew. A ***COWBOY*** approaches in the distance.)*

(Silence.)

GEORGETTE. the coffee will be ready soon

(Silence.)

RENÉ. good

(Silence.)

GEORGETTE. I overslept
so I couldn't get it brewing before you woke up

(Silence.)

RENÉ. okay

(Silence.)

GEORGETTE. I'm using a new brand
they were out of our usual brand

(Silence.)

RENÉ. happens

(Silence.)

GEORGETTE. normally I make the coffee with four scoops
you know how I do that

(Silence.)

RENÉ. right of course

(Silence.)

GEORGETTE. René

RENÉ. yes

GEORGETTE. how many scoops

do I normally make the coffee with

> *(Silence.)*

well it's four

> *(Silence.)*

but today I made it with five
so the coffee may be stronger

> *(Silence.)*

so I hope you're okay with strong coffee

RENÉ. I like strong coffee

GEORGETTE. no you don't
I like strong coffee
you like white tea

RENÉ. yummmm

> *(Silence.)*

white tea has antee-oxidants

> *(Silence.)*

GEORGETTE. well we're having coffee not white tea coffee
and strong coffee at that

> *(Silence.)*

RENÉ. okay

> *(Silence.)*
>
> *(Coffee brewing.)*

are we having any breakfast today

GEORGETTE. mmmm
I hadn't gotten there yet

> *(Bird sound.)*

RENÉ. that bird is still there

GEORGETTE. that bird is there every morning

RENÉ. it has a very large beak have you noticed

GEORGETTE. the better to clack with

RENÉ. yes every morning at the window clack clack clack

insufferable noise in the morning

GEORGETTE. well not insufferable
one could suffer it so it's not insufferable
not lacking in sufferability
we suffer it daily we do
so clearly it's not you know insuffera–

RENÉ. the cowboy is approaching

GEORGETTE. oh

RENÉ. that cowboy
in the distance
desert outlaw man
he's still out there
got a little closer
why do you suppose that is

GEORGETTE. the coffee's done do you want cream

RENÉ. I don't like this cowboy man
cigarette breath
and whiskey eyes poured over like charm
no cream I need to cut back on dairy

GEORGETTE. dairy's good for you actually I read an article

RENÉ. really

GEORGETTE. yeah new article new study
about how our arteries need dairy
for lubrication I think
arterial slip-n-slide I suppose

RENÉ. why would anyone live in a desert on purpose

GEORGETTE. he might not be from the desert
he might be from the plains or the prairies
and not just America places you know
there are cowboys in Argentina –

RENÉ. I don't care about Argentina cowboys
I care about that one there

GEORGETTE. he's far away
he can't hurt you

RENÉ. I don't think he's far away
  I think he's actually just
  very very
  short

GEORGETTE. maybeeeeeeeeee
  or he's just very far away

RENÉ. there's menace in his eyes
  I see it
  I see menace in his eyes
  if he is so far away
  how can I see menace in his eyes

>   *(Bird sound.)*

  I want to shoot that bird doorknob dead

GEORGETTE. maybe
  you can see the menace in his body language
  and you just imagine the eyes

RENÉ. can I have eggs for breakfast

GEORGETTE. we don't have any

RENÉ. okay

GEORGETTE. but I am brewing more coffee

RENÉ. the cowboy got closer again

GEORGETTE. maybe he's a vaquero

RENÉ. what's a vaquero

GEORGETTE. an Iberian cowboy

RENÉ. no this man feels
  aggressively
  Americanly male
  I don't like it

>   *(Silence.)*

>   *(**GEORGETTE** finishes her coffee and pours more coffee brews.)*

  what do we do if he gets closer

GEORGETTE. maybe the cowboy has a gun

maybe he's chasing an outlaw
maybe he is an outlaw
that could be exciting
maybe he's on the run
and the sheriff-general-man is on the hunt for him
maybe he's been riding for days
across the desert
searching for somewhere to stash the cash
to get the girl
there might be a shoot-up
at the O.K. Corral
two mustached men
guns a-blazing
the law versus the wild
Western banditry
that could be exciting

RENÉ. do we have any tea

GEORGETTE. there is no fucking tea
don't ask for tea

RENÉ. I think the cowboy is coming to our door

(Coffee overflows onto the floor.)

(The brewing noise continues to get louder.)

GEORGETTE. I'm getting more coffee

(Bird noises.)

(Coffee brewing.)

(It's all too loud, almost deafening, much louder than the normal sounds of birds or coffee brewing.)

*(**GEORGETTE** and **RENÉ** are shouting over the noise.)*

GET THE COWBOY TO SHOOT THE BIRD

RENÉ. I DON'T WANNA TALK TO THAT COWBOY
WHY DON'T WE STOCK TEA IN THE HOUSE

GEORGETTE. OH
YOU KNOW
THERE'S NO TEA
AT THE LOCAL GROCERY STORE
I'D HAVE TO DRIVE FAR FOR IT
AND THAT IS BAD FOR THE ENVIRONMENT

RENÉ. THE COWBOY APPROACHES

GEORGETTE. DON'T BE MELODRAMATIC

RENÉ. THE COWBOY APPROACHES
WHAT IF HE HAS A HORSE
I AM SCARED OF HORSES

GEORGETTE. HE DOESN'T HAVE A HORSE
WHERE WOULD HE BE KEEPING THE HORSE

RENÉ. I THINK I SHOULD GO UPSTAIRS MAYBE

GEORGETTE. WOULD YOU GET ME SOME SUGAR
FOR MY COFFEE

RENÉ. THE COWBOY HAS A HAT
I DO NOT LIKE HATS

GEORGETTE. YOU LOVE HATS

RENÉ. I DO NOT LIKE THAT HAT

GEORGETTE. SUGAR
PLEASE

> *(The **COWBOY** opens the door.)*
>
> *(Coffee stops brewing.)*
>
> *(The bird is gone.)*
>
> *(Silence.)*
>
> *(The **COWBOY** sits down at the table.)*
>
> *(Nobody acknowledges him.)*
>
> *(**RENÉ** sips at his cup.)*

RENÉ. coffee tastes terrible without cream

> *(Silence.)*

it's still pecking at the window

the bird the bird I mean
I think the coffee machine is on the fritz
the brewing sounds like bullets

> *(None of what **RENÉ** has just said is true.)*
>
> *(**GEORGETTE** offers the **COWBOY** coffee.)*

home should be quiet in the morning don't you think
like a church at night
like a meadow in winter
bird chirp a low din
tiny clink of metal spoon to china cup
grass crunch under small dog
a teapot
a chair
a cupboard

> *(**GEORGETTE** begins to undress the **COWBOY**.)*

today I'll paint I think
brush to canvass
splotches of color
color to be rendered orderly
today I'm working on
compositional precision
line curve shift corner space border
banish the smudge
I say
cover the smear
that's what I say
balance symmetry austerity
true nonsense from true clarity
the needlepoint rendering
of real objects in real space
is so much more frightening I think
strip back the excess
to get at true terror

(The **COWBOY** *is fully stripped.)*

*(***GEORGETTE*** takes his fingers and puts them inside of her.)*

(She fingers herself.)

(It is private and not for us.)

RENÉ. I want to start making tea in the mornings
I hate coffee actually actually I hate it
white tea comes in all kinds of flavors
peach mango apricot vanilla
ginger cucumber blossom berry
coffee just comes in two flavors
gravel and pavement
you say the scoop number's the thing
fewer scoops and it'll go down smooth
but I taste road regardless of the scoop number
white tea would get me excited in the mornings
I'd hop out of bed and think "oh boy tea time"
tea with bacon
tea with hash browns
tea with eggs
tea with home fries
I think that sounds tastier
so white tea in the mornings I think
no more coffee

*(***GEORGETTE*** cums.)*

(It's almost silent.)

after I paint I thought we could play some cards
pet the cat
tend the garden
prune the bushes
pick some flowers
clean the kitchen
light a fire

make some tea
read a book
do the laundry
play a record
cook a stew
have a drink
have another
wash the dishes
walk the dog
make the bed
wind the clock
go to sleep
that sorta thing

(Silence.)

GEORGETTE. this is probably as good a time as any
to announce that I've been having an affair

(Silence.)

RENÉ. oh

(Silence.)

*(**RENÉ** almost cries.)*

(Then he steadies himself.)

how
when
who
towards what

GEORGETTE. there are two houses
that stand side by side
the white house and the black house
in the white house I sat
blank and clean
funereal
patient
in the black house you slept with another woman

of course and obviously and expectedly
Great Man Cultured Man Artist Man
of course and obviously and expectedly
and in a little twitch of pity
you sent a man
a delegate
an ambassador
from the black house to the white house
like a tender ship into my waters
to mend to repair
and I took
devoured tracelessly
spinning hot desire
unmapped unlandscaped passion
flat wild undiscerning
I split your clean lines
I soiled your fine shapes
I stained the white house
a bloody pulpy carnage of color

   (Silence.)

but in my defense
your affair came first

RENÉ. right

GEORGETTE. and you were the one
who sent Paul to me

RENÉ. to comfort you

GEORGETTE. well
I *was*
comforted

   (Silence.)

RENÉ. I presumed
utter heartbreak on your part
when the news broke of my affair

so I sent a friend

GEORGETTE. you shouldn't have presumed

> *(Silence.)*

RENÉ. I'm not seeing Sheila right now

GEORGETTE. that
seems like an error on your part

RENÉ. I always told myself
only weak men wander

GEORGETTE. I don't think that's true

> *(Silence.)*

RENÉ. I scrambled things here I know that
I thought I'd go adrift in middle age
instead I've gone driftless
no vaquero life for me

GEORGETTE. vaquero life was
never really in the cards for you René

RENÉ. do you want a divorce

> *(Silence.)*

Georgette

> *(Silence.)*

do you want more coffee

GEORGETTE. yes please

> *(**RENÉ** serves **GEORGETTE** and the **COWBOY** more coffee.)*
>
> *(They all sit and drink.)*

End of Play

Jack + Jill

Book & Lyrics by Sarah Hammond
Music by Emily Goldman

JACK + JILL received its premiere production as part of the Samuel French Off Off Broadway Short Play Festival at the Classic Stage Company in New York City on August 10 & 12, 2017. The production was directed by Tyler Spicer. The associate director was Mary Jessica Colvin. The cast was as follows:

JACK .... Keith Caram
JILL... Carly Blane

JACK + JILL was originally written at NYU's Graduate Musical Theatre Writing Program. Subsequently, a concert version was performed in the New Georges Trunk Show at the Cornelia Street Cafe. Special thanks to Sam Heldt and Mallory Hawks, who first brought Jack and Jill to life in those presentations.

CHARACTERS

JACK – A boy who loves Jill.
JILL – A girl who grows up.

SETTING

A little town with a hill in California.
Then Jill's apartment back East.

TIME

Their childhood.
Then the present.

"Jack fell down and broke his crown,
and Jill came tumbling after."

(JACK and JILL run on to announce their show, gleeful and bratty.)

JACK & JILL. Welcome to the story of Jack and Jill!

(JILL blows a note on a pitch pipe, they take a breath.)

[MUSIC NO. 01 "IDENTICAL FRIENDS"]

EVERYBODY HATED JACK AND JILL.
THEY WERE THE SAME IN EVERY WAY.

JILL.

IDENTICAL HAIR,

JACK.

IDENTICAL CLOTHES,

JACK & JILL.

IDENTICAL HOPES AND FEARS

JILL.

NOBODY LIKES

JACK.

IDENTICAL FRIENDS

JACK & JILL.

BUT THEY STAYED THAT WAY FOR YEARS.

(They shift into the characters, best friends, with a casual best friend dance. A kick here, a nudge there.)

JACK.

WHEN I GET AN ITCH IN MY NOSE,
SHE SNEEZES.

JILL.

WHEN I GET A ROCK IN MY SHOE,
HE DANCES.

JACK.

> WHEN I CLOSE MY EYES AT NIGHT,
> SHE DREAMS –

JILL.

> I DREAM –

JACK.

> SHE DREAMS,

JACK.	**JILL.**
I DREAM –	HE DREAMS –

JACK & JILL.

> WE DREAM.

JILL. Do you know what else? We both wear shower shoes.

JACK & JILL.

> EVERYBODY HATED JACK AND JILL.
> THEY WERE THE SAME
> OH SO THE SAME IN EVERY WAY.

JACK. *(Defensively.)* So what?

> *(He's maybe ready to pick a fight with someone in the audience, but she pulls him back.)*

JILL. *(To him.)* Jack...

> *(To audience.)*

> WHEN I THINK A BEAUTIFUL THOUGHT,
> HE SMILES.

JACK.

> WHEN I THROW A PUNCH IN A FIGHT,
> HER FIST HURTS.

JILL.

> WHEN I GET A HOLE IN MY HEART,
> HE SIGHS.

JACK.

> I SIGH –

JILL.	**JACK.**
HE SIGHS, HE SIGHS –	OH

JILL.

> HE SEES ME
> EVEN WHEN I'M NOT IN THE ROOM.
> WE'RE THE SAME.

> *(Music ends as they drop into conversation with the audience.)*

JACK. We didn't do it on purpose –

JILL. Not on purpose –

JACK. We just seem to like –

JILL. – And/or dislike –

JACK & JILL. – All of the exact same things.

JACK. Like green. That time we figured out our favorite color was green.

JILL. I was like "My favorite color is green."

JACK. And so was mine!

JILL. And I was like "Ohmygosh! It's not!"

JACK. But it is!

JILL. Was. That's when we were four.

JACK. Now our favorite color is black.

JILL. Black.

JACK. Black.

JACK & JILL. We are older now. So.

JACK. People don't understand.

JILL. People don't get us.

JACK. Last year we were vegetarians, but now we eat chicken.

JILL. *(Fiercely, aside to audience.)* He is my exact carbon copy in boy form.

JACK. When we eat chicken, I take one leg –

JILL. And I take the other.

JACK. The only thing we can't split –

JILL. The only thing we can't split –

JACK & JILL. – Is the egg!

> *(They put on bookbags, shifting into a scene.)*

JILL. School.

JACK. School.

JILL. Guess what I'm thinking.

JACK. Skip school.

JILL. *(Relieved.)* Yes.

JACK. I already packed a picnic.

JILL. How did you know?

JACK. Guess what I'm thinking.

[MUSIC NO. 02 "WHAT I LIKE ABOUT JACK"]

JILL. The hill.

JACK. I thought we could climb the hill.

JILL. What's up your sleeve?

JACK. I wanna see if we can see the ocean today.

> *(They go. He leads the way, chattering the whole time. She follows, meandering, lost in her own happy thoughts.)*

JILL.
> SKIP MATH, SAYS JACK.
> BE WISE, SAYS JACK.

JACK. To the top!

JILL.
> AND JACK NEVER CRIES,

JACK. C'mon.

JILL.
> NOT JACK.
> HE PARTS HIS HAIR ON THE RIGHT LIKE ME
> HE READS MARK TWAIN EVERY NIGHT LIKE ME
> SOMETIMES IT'S LIKE WE'RE SHARING THE SAME BRAIN
> SOMETIMES.

JACK. Are you listening?

JILL.
> BUT THAT'S

JACK. Jill.

JILL.

    WHAT I LIKE.

JACK. Catch up.

JILL.

    YEAH THAT'S

JACK. C'mon.

JILL.

    WHAT I LIKE

JACK. Come on.

JILL.

    ABOUT JACK.

JACK. You know, you and me are really lucky.

JILL.

    BE SMART, SAYS JACK.

    CLIMB HIGH, SAYS JACK.

JACK. It's rare when people click like us.

JILL.

    RIGHT UP TO THE SKY,

JACK. Like we do.

JILL.

    GOES JACK.

    IT'S IMPORTANT, HE SAYS, WHEN WE CLIMB THE HILL,

    IT'S IMPORTANT TO SEE THE HORIZON, JILL.

    LOOKING AT HIM IS LIKE LOOKING RIGHT INTO A

       MIRROR

    BUT HE'S

    ...a person.

JACK. Also.

JILL.

    AND THAT'S

JACK. When we get our braces off.

JILL.

    WHAT I LIKE

JACK. We should smile more.

JILL.

    YEAH THAT'S

JACK. *(Arriving at top of hill.)* Ah.

JILL.

    WHAT I LIKE

JACK. *Here* we are.

JILL.

    ABOUT JACK.

JACK. Sit.

      (He unpacks a picnic. She doesn't sit yet.)

JILL.

    MY THOUGHTS ARE HIS THOUGHTS
    AND HIS THOUGHTS ARE MINE.
    WE ALWAYS THINK RIGHT THOUGHTS,
    WE ALWAYS AGREE.
    THAT'S WHAT YOU WANT IN A FRIEND, RIGHT?
    THAT'S WHAT YOU WANT IN A FRIEND?
    SOMEONE WITH WHOM YOU AGREE.

JACK. Now we can see each other in the pond. Hi. Look at the lavender growing in the grass. We should bring some back for your mom. Smell it. Nice, huh?

      (She sits.)

JILL.

    IT'S GOOD WITH JACK.
    SO NICE WITH JACK.
    NO NEED TO THINK TWICE
    WITH JACK.
    WE CLIMB THE HILL TO THE VERY TOP.
    HE KICKS AT THE ROCKS AND WE WATCH THEM DROP.
    SOMETIMES IT'S LIKE WE'RE WEARING THE SAME SKIN
    SOMETIMES.
    AND THAT'S WHAT I LIKE,
    YEAH THAT'S WHAT I LIKE
    ABOUT JACK.

JACK. – And I'd like to marry you if you don't mind.

JILL. What?!

      (The song buttons and he continues, unphased.)

JACK. I'd like to marry you. Not now, but eventually. Of course, we are only twelve. But life doesn't have a lot of surprises in it, and I just don't think that anybody else in the world will ever understand me like you do, and I think that you feel the same, and so it seems only natural that after we go to the University of California at Berkley, and after we get our degrees in plate tectonics, after *that* we should probably get married. So that then we can have the same house during graduate school. Right?

JILL. Oh.

JACK. Guess what I'm thinking.

JILL. *(Really alarmed.)* I have no idea. I have no idea what you're thinking.

JACK. That's okay.

> *(Pause.)*

> *(Quietly.)* Also because I love you.

JILL. *(Also quietly.)* Oh.

JACK. I meant to say that first.

JILL. That's okay, Jack.

> *(He takes her hand.)*

[MUSIC NO. 03 "I FALL"]

JACK.

> WHEN YOU THINK A BEAUTIFUL THOUGHT,
> I SMILE.
> AND I KNOW THAT WE ARE BOTH SO VERY
> VERY YOUNG
> BUT WHEN I LOOK INTO YOUR EYES,
> I FALL

JILL.

> YOU FALL?

JACK.

> I FALL!
> I FALL!

> *(He leans across and kisses her.)*

JACK. Do you...?

> *(She doesn't.)*

JILL. Jack.

JACK. Jill?

JILL. Jack, um... *Um.*

JACK. *(Getting it.)* Oh.

JILL. I don't think...

JACK. Oh.

Okay.

> *(He pats her hand. He lets go of her hand.)*

Gosh, it's.

Should we try to get to school in time for second period?

> *(He shrugs on his bookbag and goes.)*
>
> *(She stays.)*
>
> *(She puts down her bookbag.)*

JILL. *(Simply, to the audience.)* Then, of course, there is the thing of growing up...

> *(Looking around at her apartment.)*

One day, there you are in your own adult life. Which is not quite the life you pictured, is it? Well, whose is. And still, it's yours.

[MUSIC NO. 04 "JILL BREAKS AN EGG"]

A chair. Butter and toast. Breakfast in your own apartment.

> *(JILL ages fifteen years.)*
>
> *(Maybe lights come up on a tableau of her adult life. The white drywall of an apartment, a pile of books, a window, venetian blinds, a houseplant surrounded by a clutter of teacups, a metal trash can covered in magnets, and beside JILL, a little stool with the accoutrements of breakfast: coffee, apple*

slices, jam, butter, toast, an egg.)

(Or maybe we just see **JILL** *tidying a blanket and looking out an invisible window, happy with the life she built, but keenly aware of what's missing.)*

JILL MAKES
AN EGG,
JILL BREAKS
THE SHELL,
SHE BREAKS
THE SHELL ON THE PAN.
JILL MAKES
BREAKFAST IN JULY
IN HER STUDIO
ON NORTH STREET.

THE MORNING IS GOOD,
WHEN SHE WAKES UP WITH THE RADIO,
WANDERS ROUND THE STUDIO
ON NORTH STREET.

SHE BREAKS
THE EGG,
SHE BREAKS
THE SHELL ON THE PAN.
IF ONLY THERE IS ALWAYS BREAKFAST.
IF ONLY THERE ARE ALWAYS MORNINGS
AND WINDOWS AND STORM CLOUDS,
HILLTOPS
JUST ROUND THE BEND.
IF ONLY BEGINNINGS
DID NOT NEED TO END.

SHE BREAKS THE EGG,
AND SOMETHING NEW FILLS UP THE ROOM

A FLASH OF JACK
OF ONCE UPON A TIME
WHEN HE WAS JACK
AND SHE WAS JILL.

(**JACK** *enters, returning to his picnic spot, always at the top of the hill. A memory.*)

(*She looks.*)

(*She looks and looks.*)

End of Play

Sir

Jahna Ferron-Smith

SIR was produced as part of the Samuel French Off Off Broadway Short Play Festival at the Classic Stage Company in New York City on August 9, 2017. The production was directed by Matt Dickson. The cast was as follows:

CHRIS . . . . Max Reinhardsen
LEILA . . . . Akiyaa Wilson

CHARACTERS

CHRIS – Twenty-seven. A White man.
LEILA – Twenty-seven. A Black woman.

SETTING

Driving in Chris' car, from New York to New Jersey for Thanksgiving.

TIME

Present.

AUTHOR'S NOTES

A forward slash / indicates an interruption in conversation.

Any and all text within parentheses is not meant to be spoken.

Phone conversation from Carol, Jim, and Donnie should be heard but those family members should not be seen.

"Lei" is pronounced "Lay."

*(**CHRIS** and **LEILA** are driving in a car. The radio starts to go to static. **LEILA** goes to plug in her phone.)*

(It's dead.)

LEILA. Baby, did you bring your charger?

CHRIS. It's in my bag. In the trunk.

LEILA. What's yours at?

*(**CHRIS** checks his phone.)*

CHRIS. Fifteen percent.

LEILA. Never mind.

(Companionable silence.)

*(**LEILA** squeezes **CHRIS**' lower thigh.)*

(She leaves her hand there.)

I love you so much.

CHRIS. I love you too.

(Driving.)

LEILA. Oh! Did you – uh – did you get my email.

CHRIS. *(Laughing a little.)* Yes, I got your email.

LEILA. What – why are you laughing?

CHRIS. I'm not!

LEILA. Real mature, Chris.

CHRIS. Your lead-in was weird –

LEILA. Well, I'm feeling vulnerable –

CHRIS. I'm feeling vulnerable!

LEILA. Okay!

(Lull.)

CHRIS. I'm not making fun. I'm (uncomfortable)...this is new. For me.

LEILA. I know.

> (**CHRIS** *takes her hand and kisses the back.*)
> (*He drives.*)

Did you check out the links?

CHRIS. I was at work.

LEILA. You work from home.

CHRIS. I was working – I was WORKING – it's a company computer – I didn't want them to find anything.

> (**LEILA** *is mad.*)

And – FINE – maybe I did feel a little blindsided when my girlfriend asked me to be violent toward her during sex –

LEILA. Is it weird for you? Do you think this is weird?

CHRIS. ...

LEILA. Do you think I'm / weird?

CHRIS. Absolutely not – I really am trying to be sensitive.

> (*Moment.*)

Wait, are you seriously mad at me right now?

LEILA. (*Clearly mad.*) I'm not mad.

CHRIS. Please don't do that, okay? I don't want to walk into Thanksgiving – at my PARENTS' HOUSE with...this... energy.

LEILA. (*"Not mad."*) What energy?

CHRIS. Just...like...my little sister is there.

LEILA. So you think that somehow, through some bizarre sort of energetic osmosis, your sister is going to know that we're considering BDSM? – Which – apparently – we're not because you can't even be bothered to check out the links.

CHRIS. That's not fair –

LEILA. It's not like I asked you to punch me in the face while we fuck –

CHRIS. Please don't yell.

LEILA. (*Calmer.*) Let's speak in intentions.

CHRIS. Okay.

LEILA. It was not my intention to blindside you with anything. It *was* my intention to bring to your attention a carefully researched desire to explore bondage, dominance, and sadomasochism – one that I've had for a long time now –

CHRIS. Then, why is this the first time I'm hearing about it –

(**LEILA** *gives* **CHRIS** *a "tread lightly" look.*)

LEILA. It IS my intention to explore if this is a dynamic you could get into.

CHRIS. My intention was not to offend... I'm nervous that this could become problematic, really, really quickly – I'm going to switch to "I feels" now. /

LEILA. Go for it.

CHRIS. Is that okay?

LEILA. The podcast said we could switch as needed.

CHRIS. Okay: I feel uncomfortable at the prospect of being violent toward you. I feel it perpetuates an unhealthy narrative – one that others already assume we're included in. I don't want to prove them right –

LEILA. This isn't about proving anything to anyone – this is about you and me: the only two people in this relationship.

CHRIS. I FEEL like it's demeaning.

LEILA. Because I'm black?

CHRIS. No! – Well, yes – Just – you want me – ME – to tie you up and WHIP you?

LEILA. *(Beat.)* We would work up to that.

CHRIS. I don't know –

LEILA. But you've never tried it.

CHRIS. *(Beat.)* I have tried it. Once.

LEILA. With Rebecca?

(**CHRIS**'*phone begins to ring.*)

CHRIS. Don't look at me like that, she was my only other long-term girlfriend and these things require a lot of trust –

LEILA. So you trusted your relationship with white Rebecca enough to punch HER in the face while fucking, but ME –

CHRIS. Could you please stop using that example; it's weakening your argument –

LEILA. WHAT IF I WANT TO BE PUNCHED, CHRIS?! Do you trust THIS relationship that much?

> (**CHRIS** *finally answers the phone on speakerphone.*)

CHRIS. Hi Mom, we're about six minutes –

CAROL. *(Voice-over.)* Hi sweetie, how are you?

CHRIS. I'm good – we're about –

CAROL. *(Voice-over.)* Is Leila with you?

CHRIS. She's right next to me –

CAROL. *(Voice-over.)* Tell her I say hi!

CHRIS. We're gonna be there so soon, you could just –

CAROL. *(Voice-over.)* Tell her now, please, I don't want to seem rude.

CHRIS. *(To* **LEILA.***)* My mother says "hi."

CAROL. *(Voice-over.)* Not like that!

CHRIS. *(To* **LEILA** *again, begrudgingly chipper.)* My mother says "hi!"

LEILA. *(Clearly annoyed.)* Hi Carol.

CHRIS. She says "hi" –

LEILA. Not like that!

CHRIS. *(To* **LEILA.***)* That's how you said it –
(To Carol, begrudgingly enthusiastic.) She says, "hi!" – Listen, Mom, I don't want to get a ticket, did you need something??

CAROL. *(Voice-over.)* Oh no, just checking in.

CHRIS. Right. So, we'll be there in five minutes now –

JIM. *(Voice-over.)* How long?

CAROL. *(Voice-over.)* They'll be here in five minutes.

JIM. *(Voice-over.)* That's not long at all!

CAROL. *(Voice-over.)* Not. It's not!

JIM. *(Voice-over.)* Hi Chris.

CAROL. *(Voice-over. To* **CHRIS**.*)* Your father says "hi!"

CHRIS. Hi Dad – Mom, I have to go –

CAROL. *(Voice-over.)* Do you want to speak to your father?

DONNIE. *(Voice-over.)* Is that Chris?

CAROL. *(Voice-over. To Donnie.)* Yes!

    (To **CHRIS**.*)* Uncle Donnie's here.

> *(***CHRIS*** *sighs.* **LEILA** *closes her eyes to try to calm her rage.)*

CHRIS. I'm gonna hang up now, but we'll be there soon... okay...okay...yes...okay, yeah... Four minutes...love you...love you...bye.

> *(***CHRIS*** *hangs up.)*

LEILA. You said – assured me – Uncle Donnie wasn't going to be here.

CHRIS. He's my father's only remaining sibling –

LEILA. He voted for Trump.

CHRIS. And he just got out of the hospital.

LEILA. *(Beat.)* He voted for Trump.

CHRIS. We'll sit on the opposite side of the table.

LEILA. It's only a six-person table.

CHRIS. Well, just *try* to keep an open mind. We're doing that about a lot of things tonight, so...

> *(***CHRIS*** *drives.)*

Would you...would you, like, call me "master"?

LEILA. There are plenty of other comparable, authoritative titles that don't evoke slave imagery –

CHRIS. Like what?

LEILA. ...Sir?

CHRIS. ...

LEILA. Give me your phone, I'll look some up.

CHRIS. RIGHT HERE – right here: I don't want anything even hinting at that questionable energy anywhere near our sex life –

LEILA. IT'S ALREADY HERE. I'm black. You're white. This is America. Regardless of whether or not we decide to do this, that dynamic – that "narrative" – is still there –

CHRIS. SO WHY ARE WE INDULGING IT?

LEILA. THIS IS DIFFERENT – all of the "vanilla" sex –

    (**CHRIS** *looks hurt.*)

"NON-PLAY" – "non-play" beautiful, wonderful sex we have, is not going to make the American-sociopolitical- interracial-bullshit any less present –

CHRIS. Is it bullshit? Because it feels VERY real. The way you talk about how the "good ol' boys" exclude you at work, feels very real. When someone whispers to you, "I hope you die" when we walk down a crowded street and you squeeze my hand: that feels very real.

LEILA. A. I don't need you to "protect" me / –

CHRIS. "Protect you" – ARE YOU SERIOUS?

LEILA. And, B. I'm CHOOSING this.

CHRIS. BUT WHERE'S THE LINE, LEI? You're fine with "Sir," but not "Master"? – Both of which are equally cringe-worthy to me. Am I allowed to tell you "you deserve it" while gagged *and* bound? Or just gagged?

LEILA. We'd establish rules.

CHRIS. What if I say the wrong thing?

LEILA. *(Beat.)* Like what?

CHRIS. That look: I never want to make you feel like you have to give me that look. Ever. Especially while I'm inside you.

LEILA. Look, I'm not saying we ignore the bullshit, but I'm for damn sure not going to let that dictate what's an appropriate form of sexual self-expression. I'm not going to let that control how I explore my body because now, I *get to* have control over my body.

(They've pulled into the front drive of Carol's house. They get out.)

Please don't think I take this lightly. I'm *asking* for this – I don't need to be coddled or treated differently than White Rebecca –

*(**CHRIS** rings the doorbell.)*

CHRIS. BUT YOU *ARE* DIFFERENT. Isn't that part of your point?

LEILA. ...

CHRIS. I mean, you still call her "White Rebecca"!! Do *you* trust this relationship enough to do this?

(Carol opens the front door.)

End of Play

Square Footage

Jessica Moss

SQUARE FOOTAGE was produced by Theatre Mischief as part of the Samuel French Off Off Broadway Short Play Festival at the Classic Stage Company in New York City on August 8, 2017. The production was directed by Eric Harper and Jessica Moss. The cast was as follows:

NATE . . . . Eric Harper

MAGGIE . . . . Jessica Moss

Earlier productions of the play were produced as part of the Tomo Suru About Love Festival in Vancouver, BC, in June 2016; and the This is Water Festival in College Station, Texas, in February 2017.

CHARACTERS

NATE – dating Maggie.
MAGGIE – dating Nate.
Both in their late twenties to late thirties.
Both fast talkers.
Both in love. Whatever that means. Right?

SETTING

Nate's apartment. Which is now Maggie and Nate's apartment. Small.
(There is no set).

TIME

Now.

AUTHOR'S NOTES

A "/" indicates the point of interruption where the following line begins
(à la Caryl Churchill).

Words in square brackets [like these] are intended but not spoken aloud.

The "booms" were sound effects that increasingly got louder in the
original production.

And go fast.

Casting Note

If you'd like to do this play with two men, two women, or two gender
non-conforming individuals, feel free! Change Nate's name to "Nia,"
or Maggie's name to "Matty," if you'd like, or use names of your own
choosing that start with an "N" and an "M."

(Fast lights up.)

*(**NATE** and **MAGGIE** are pressed up against each other. They are in a box of light about two feet by two feet [or whatever size allows us to clearly see both actors while leaving them with virtually no space and forcing them to always be in total physical contact].)*

*(This is their apartment. Well, it was **NATE**'s apartment. And **MAGGIE** just moved in.)*

(And man, it is small.)

(You don't need any props or set. You don't need to do any realistic miming. It's probably better if you don't. Find a theatrical language for them to do all the things they do, pressed up against each other and in this tiny box of light that is their apartment.)

(Very fast-paced.)

NATE. Well!

MAGGIE. Here we are!

NATE & MAGGIE. EEEEEEEEEE!!

MAGGIE. This is so ex / citing!

NATE. BIG step!

MAGGIE. What?

NATE. Exciting! I mean, my place is small.

MAGGIE. Yes.

NATE. But –

MAGGIE. We'll make it work.

NATE. Exactly.

MAGGIE. We'll just...make it work.

> *(They look around the apartment, still smiling.)*

MAGGIE. I mean / it's very small!

NATE. It's small though, yeah.

MAGGIE. It didn't seem this small. When I would sleep over.

NATE. Well, only one person was living here.

MAGGIE. Yes, but –

NATE. Only one person's stuff.

MAGGIE. But I sold. All my stuff.

NATE. You sold most. / Of your stuff.

MAGGIE. I sold anything that really takes up space, I just brought my clothes and books, and my computer, and a few, I mean, a few kitchen things that you didn't have, and the things I need –

NATE. And the bed.

> *(They look at the bed.)*
>
> *(Boom.)*

MAGGIE. Yeah, but that's –

NATE. No, I love that.

MAGGIE. It's a good piece of furniture. We should hold on to that.

NATE. And we did.

> *(Boom.)*

MAGGIE. I mean...you just had your Ikea thing.

NATE. Yes.

MAGGIE. This is, this is a real piece of furniture. It's an antique. We're going to have this forever.

NATE. Forever?

> *(BOOM.)*

MAGGIE. It's an investment. It's a grown-up piece of furniture, and –

NATE. And it's here! It's really here. Like right smack in the / middle of the room.

MAGGIE. Well, it needs a better spot, it needs to go somewhere, / we just need to find the right place for it.

NATE. You're right, you're right, it's fine, / I'm just so happy you're here.

MAGGIE. Who said it wasn't fine I'M HAPPY I'M HERE TOO!

(They embrace. They happily hold each other.)

NATE. It will be fine.

MAGGIE. Yeah… Can you move the bed?

NATE. Ugh.

MAGGIE. Don't ugh me, it's been three months.

NATE. I know, you've told me that every day / since you moved here.

MAGGIE. I just think it will give us more / space.

NATE. Space, right.

(Beat. They look at each other.)

MAGGIE. What?

NATE. Nothing.

MAGGIE. No, just, / what?

NATE. I don't know, / I just –

MAGGIE. You don't like it.

NATE. It's just very big.

MAGGIE. It will be better when it's not positioned like that, it needs to go in a corner.

NATE. But that means I don't get a side table, / and I have to crawl over you to get in and out.

MAGGIE. We'll get a little light on the wall and a a a shelf thing.

NATE. I have to crawl over you to get in and out. Look.

MAGGIE. No I don't want to / look.

NATE. You should see.

MAGGIE. I don't – ughghghg…

(They get into the bed.)

NATE. See?

MAGGIE. Yeah, I mean, / I understand, but I think it's going to be better – I, uggghhh.

NATE. Middle of the night, I need to pee, or drink water – *(He climbs over her.)* or whatever, and I have to do all of this, like ugghg, oh, look at me.

> (**NATE** *makes a big show of climbing over her and accidentally smacks* **MAGGIE** *in the eye.*)

MAGGIE. *(Her eye.)* OW!

NATE. You see?

MAGGIE. OWWWW!

NATE. Oh, shit.

MAGGIE. I'm going to have a black eye!

NATE. I'm sorry. Put a steak on it!

MAGGIE. Why did you do that?

NATE. Frozen peas?

MAGGIE. Owwwww!

NATE. It wasn't on purpose, / you know I wouldn't do that on purpose.

MAGGIE. Why did you have to demonstrate it when I told you I know?

NATE. You're not going to tell people that I gave you a black eye, are you? You're not going to phrase it that way when people ask, are you, you'll tell them how it actually was?

MAGGIE. Oh god it really hurts!

NATE. I'm sorry! God, that was ages ago, how long are you going to rub that in my face?

MAGGIE. You did hit me in the / eye.

NATE. BY ACCIDENT.

MAGGIE. You wouldn't have hit me in the eye if we weren't always on top of each other like this.

NATE. Do you want to get a bigger place? Because a bigger place will be a lot more money, it will be so much more money.

MAGGIE. I know.

NATE. Just so much more money.

MAGGIE. I knowwwww.

NATE. And I mean I thought the whole point of moving in together was to save money.

MAGGIE. I thought the whole point of moving in together was that we wanted to move in together. Was this just a / financial decision for you?

NATE. NO. No.

MAGGIE. Because I thought…and I mean you won't even try the bed somewhere else, which I've been saying for ages. You won't even try it. You say you're okay for me to move in here, which you obviously aren't, and now I find out it was just for you to save money, and you won't even try the thing that could maybe make our lives a little bit better.

NATE. It's not that I don't want to try to move the bed, it's that I can't move it all myself, you have to help.

MAGGIE. I will.

NATE. Will you?

MAGGIE. Why are you talking / to me like that, of course I'll help.

NATE. I'm not talking to you like anything, but you want to move the bed so let's move it.

MAGGIE. Or we could just…not move it. We could just. Break up.

NATE. …Is that what you / want?

MAGGIE. I don't know. It seems though that there isn't room in your…life. For me. And you won't even try to make the room, so…

NATE. I said I would make the room, we can move the stupid bed –

MAGGIE. That's not what I mean, and it's not stupid, it's an antique!

NATE. Well it weighs a million frigging pounds, so I can't do it by myself.

MAGGIE. I SAID I WOULD HELP YOU!

(BOOM.)

(They glare at each other.)

NATE. Yup, great, well, let's move it. Great.

(**NATE** *gets into position to move it.*)

Do you have your end?

MAGGIE. No, I can't, there isn't room for me to bend so I can't to the bottom.

NATE. Squat, you have to squat.

MAGGIE. I'm not strong enough squatting, I have to do it from bent over / but there isn't enough room for me to bend over.

NATE. You're gonna break your back doing it that way, you have to use your legs.

MAGGIE. My back is stronger than my – okay, I'm under it.

(She is.)

NATE. Are you?

MAGGIE. Yes.

NATE. Really?

MAGGIE. Yes!

NATE. This isn't like a thing where you say you're helping but you're just pretending to help, you aren't actually carrying any weight?

(**MAGGIE** *bites her lip.*)

Hellooooo?

MAGGIE. When have I ever done that?

NATE. I don't know, I'm just saying.

MAGGIE. You shouldn't just say –

NATE. Fine. FINE. Do you want to move the bed?

MAGGIE. YES ALL I'VE WANTED FOR SIX MONTHS IS TO / MOVE THE BED.

NATE. I THOUGHT ALL YOU WANTED WAS TO LIVE WITH ME AND ME NOT HIT YOU IN THE FACE.

NATE & MAGGIE. UGHGHGHGHG!

> *(Furiously, they lower themselves down and try to pick up the bed.)*

> *(There really isn't enough space to do this.)*

Ugghghgghg.

> *(It's super heavy and doesn't budge.)*

> *(**MAGGIE** stands up and shakes her arms.)*

> *(**NATE** looks at her.)*

> *(**MAGGIE** immediately reassumes her position.)*

> *(They inhale and try again.)*

Ughghghghghghghg.

> *(They get it the tiniest bit off the ground and then have to put it down.)*

> *(Dammit.)*

> *(They stretch, they amp themselves up, they get ready to try again.)*

> *(They assume the positions and –)*

UGHGHGUGHGHGUGUGUGUGUGUGUGUGUGUG UGG!!!!

> *(They get it up!)*

> *(Oh god, it's moving!)*

> *(They circle around each other.)*

MAGGIE. Left.

NATE. Left?

MAGGIE. The way we're / going.

NATE. That's right, you mean right. Uggghghghggh!

NATE & MAGGIE. Ughghghghghghghg!

> *(They put the bed down in its new home.)*

> *(And then, together, they take an enormous step away from each other.)*

> *(There's a whooooosh sound. The stage lights up.)*

(There is suddenly a lot of space between and around them.)

NATE. Wow!

MAGGIE. I know!

NATE. It worked!

MAGGIE. I know!

NATE. You were right!

> *(Cupping his hands around his mouth and calling to her.)*

Helloooooo!

MAGGIE. *(Copying him.)* Hellooooo!!

NATE. Howwww are youuuuuu??

MAGGIE. Howwwww's the weatherrrr over therrrrrreee??

> *(They laugh.)*
>
> *(They spread their arms.)*
>
> *(They twist back and forth, taking up as much space as possible.)*

NATE. We could play basketball in here.

MAGGIE. We could have dance parties in here.

NATE. We could build a smaller apartment and rent it out, in here!

MAGGIE. Yes!

NATE. We could have a million beds and put them up everywhere, / a whole apartment full of beds!

MAGGIE. Yes! Yes!

NATE. And I see you, with the space around you, it's like I can actually see you, the way you are. Oh Maggie.

MAGGIE. Nate...

NATE. Maggie...oh...

> *(They love each other in the space. Then:)*

Are you okay over there?

MAGGIE. Yeah, I mean...yeah. Are you?

NATE. Yeah? It's kind of... / spooky?

MAGGIE. Eerie? Yes / that's it.

NATE. Yeah. I mean it's nice, but...

(They are still. They listen.)

MAGGIE. Do you hear / the wind?

NATE. I do hear the wind. It's weird.

MAGGIE. It's like there's... I mean this will sound crazy –

NATE. No, say it, / I think –

MAGGIE. It's almost as if there's...too...much...space? / Is that crazy?

NATE. I WAS JUST THINKING THE – NO, that's not crazy at all!

MAGGIE. There's too much, right?

NATE. My god, I miss you so much.

MAGGIE. I miss you too.

(They reach for each other. They are nowhere near.)

NATE. I just want to be so close to you.

MAGGIE. All the time.

NATE. Oh Maggie.

MAGGIE. Nate...

(Reach reach reach.)

NATE. I couldn't see you. We were too...close up. I need the space to love you, I need the space to put the love in, but now you're [there]...and I need you [here].

MAGGIE. Well could we...?

(She takes a step toward him.)

NATE. Oh!

(He takes one toward her.)

(They cautiously do this, getting closer together.)

MAGGIE. You're not going to punch me in the / face again, are you?

NATE. No, I'm not going to – can you just, come here.

> *(They are close, close enough for their fingers to touch.)*

> *(Which they do.)*

MAGGIE. Oh...

> *(And then they embrace. As close as they were when the apartment was wee.)*

> *(The lights circle in on them.)*

NATE. It looks better now.

MAGGIE. I know, right?

NATE. Looks like...home.

> *(Happy happy warm warm warm.)*

MAGGIE. It's still frigging small though –

> *(A fast blackout interrupts **MAGGIE**'s last line.)*

End of Play

this movie

Amanda Keating

THIS MOVIE was produced as part of EST/Youngblood's Holiday Brunch at Ensemble Studio Theatre in New York City on December 4, 2016. The production was directed by Lily Riopelle. The cast was as follows:

STUART . . . . Jacob Perkins
JOANIE . . . . Chet Siegel

THIS MOVIE was produced as part of the Samuel French Off Off Broadway Short Play Festival at the Classic Stage Company in New York City on August 9, 2017. The production was directed by Lily Riopelle. The cast was as follows:

STUART . . . . Will Dagger
JOANIE . . . . Rachel Sachnoff

CHARACTERS

STUART – Twenty-seven, male.
JOANIE – Twenty-two, female.

SETTING

A movie theater in Western Massachusetts.

TIME

Now, Thanksgiving Day.

AUTHOR'S NOTES

Notes on Punctuation:

lowercase words that begin sentences are quietly minimized.

Mid-sentence Uppercase Words are intentionally articulated.

Italics are pointedly emphasized.

ALL CAPS are uncontrollably emphasized.

Mid-sentence end-stop punctuation (like a period) is a break in thought or rhythm.

Mid-sentence (parentheticals) are thought but not spoken.

Lack of punctuation at the end of a sentence is a sign of uncertainty or possible continuation

Slashes / are interruptions.

(An empty movie theater. Thanksgiving Day, the early matinee. Before the movie has started it's empty, but some kind of pre-previews are rolling on the screen – you know like the weird commercials for the movie theater that they show before the regular previews start.)

(Long stillness.)

(Um. Is this the play? Is this that play? The one in the movie theater? Uhh, The Film*?* The Flick*? Is that what it's –)*

(Oh wait here's someone something's happening.)

*(***STUART*** appears with a bag of popcorn. He watches the pre-previews and looks at the seats. He thinks about where to sit for a while and then decides. He goes and sits there. He watches the pre-previews. He eats some popcorn, careful not to eat too much before the movie has started. He takes off his coat, his scarf, his hat, his mittens, his gloves.)*

(Is anyone else coming to this movie? **STUART** *settles into the reality of this question as the lights dim a little and the regular previews begin.* He watches them roll when:)*

*(***JOANIE*** appears with a backpack and a vast array of snacks. Huge soda. Huge popcorn. Some Mike and Ikes or some Whoppers in the particular packaging you can only get in the*

---

*A license to produce *this movie* does not include a performance license for any third-party or copyrighted material. Licensees should create an original video reel or use videos in the public domain.

*movie theater. She knows right where to sit
when she comes in and she goes there. She sees*
STUART.*)*

*(She takes off her coat, her scarf, her hat, her
mittens, her gloves, all while balancing her
many snacks.* **STUART** *hears her and they
acknowledge each other as she sits.)*

*(***STUART** *watches the preview roll.* **JOANIE** *half-
watches the preview, half-watches* **STUART**.
Once this first preview is over:)

JOANIE. Hi

> *(***STUART** *hears her but does not respond.)*

Happy Thanksgiving

> *(***STUART** *hears her but does not respond.)*

HELLO HAPPY THANKSGIVING

> *(***STUART** *turns. Is she talking to me? He smiles
> politely, maybe waves a little.)*

STUART. thanks you too

> *(***STUART** *smiles at* **JOANIE**. *She just looks at
> him. After a moment, he turns back to the
> preview and eats popcorn, but is careful not
> to eat too much before the movie starts.* **JOANIE**
> *watches him as he watches the preview. After
> a bit:)*

JOANIE. So. What's wrong with you?

> *(***STUART** *looks around – she's talking to me
> right? There's no one else here, uhhh.)*

STUART. I'm sorry?

JOANIE. I said what's wrong

STUART. Um

JOANIE. You're at the 11:45 a.m. matinee alone on Thanksgiving
Day I assume that means there's something wrong like
with you or with your life situation or with your family like

you hate them or they're dead or just like far away so I'm just curious

STUART. Ha, um. nothing? really, I just came for the uh. Early Matinee and then I'm going to my um. Having Thanksgiving with my. Parents, so.

(*JOANIE watches him.*)

Later today I'll go after the movie

JOANIE. Oh. Ok.

(*She eats some of her food and drinks some of her giant soda.* STUART *turns back and watches the preview. Is she crazy? Is she going to kill me? Maybe I should go…*)

Well I hate my family and also I hate Thanksgiving. We have it at my grandma's *every year* and *every year* she prepares all the food two to three months in advance and freezes it and then puts it directly from the freezer into the oven so that the middle is frozen but the edges are somehow both gelatinous and burned as fuck. it's usually just me my mom my brother and my uncle because my dad is dead but my uncle comes late like we've all sat down to eat and he's drunk and he wears a kilt but it has this weird slit in the middle so you can see his dick and my mom just keeps leaving every ten minutes to smoke cigarettes on the back porch and my little brother well my little brother is disabled like he has a disability? so usually I just sit with him and like read but this year this year he um

(*STUART turns and looks at her.*)

he goes to this like special school now and they do Thanksgiving there so he's not gonna be there. so I came here, I actually saw this movie two weeks ago (I come to the movies a lot) but I don't even care I'm gonna watch this movie and then

(*Conspiratorially.*) I'm Gonna Sneak Into Other Movies All. Day.

(Something happens in the preview and they look at the screen.)

JOANIE. Do you ever do that?

STUART. what

JOANIE. Sneak into movies all day

STUART. no I've never done that

JOANIE. Well you should try it sometime. It's empowering and also easy to do it in this theater most of the guys who work here are meth heads and I know that for a fact because I used to have to drop my ex-boyfriend off at the methadone clinic and I've *seen these guys there.*

*(**JOANIE** starts rooting through her bag.)*

STUART. What's wrong with your brother

JOANIE. What?

STUART. You said he has a disability, so / what's

JOANIE. Right I said he has a disability I didn't say there was something *wrong with him*

STUART. Oh. / Sorry

JOANIE. He has PDD-NOS which is Pervasive Developmental Disorder Not Otherwise Specified which is a type of Autism that is considered mild but it is still a disability and he also has some bad physical problems like he has epilepsy and is overweight and is in a wheelchair

STUART. Sorry

JOANIE. Don't be sorry he is my favorite person

*(**STUART** nods and looks back at the screen. **JOANIE** watches him and eats her popcorn. After a moment she gets up and gathers her stuff. **STUART** hears it happening but doesn't look back. Once she's got everything, she walks down the aisle toward him, then scoots down the row he's sitting in. He watches her.)*

Do you want some of my food

STUART. I'm / ok

JOANIE. I got extra I always bring extra and I also brought food from outside like do you want a burger

STUART. A burger?

JOANIE. *(Pulling a burger out of her bag.)* It's from Wendy's

> *(**STUART** looks at it.)*

I didn't like roofie it or anything here

STUART. um

JOANIE. *(A real plea.)* I have a problem with impulse purchases and you're here so it would be awesome if you just had some of this

STUART. *(Sensing this is important to her.)* Ok.

> *(She hands him a burger and sits down next to him. They both unwrap their burgers.* **STUART** *looks at his.)*

Do you have ketchup?

JOANIE. Of course

> *(**JOANIE** hands **STUART** ketchup; he puts it on his burger.)*

I'm Joan. But everyone calls me Joanie. Which is a stupid name that I hate.

STUART. Oh. I'm sorry

JOANIE. What's your name?

STUART. Stuart

JOANIE. Hi Stuart

STUART. Hi

JOANIE. Are you from town?

STUART. Yeah

JOANIE. I don't remember you from high school

STUART. Most people don't

JOANIE. I remember everything

STUART. Um. Well when did you graduate

JOANIE. Four years ago. I've been at HCC not because I'm dumb I actually got Straight A's in school but I'm saving

money by getting my Associates and then I'll go to a
better school with fewer *idiots* and I also work at Allen
Vacuum Repair and Filters to make money

STUART. Oh so you know Andy

JOANIE. Um yeah obviously he owns it and is my boss and
Best Friend

STUART. I went to high school with Andy we were the same
/ year

JOANIE. Oh ok so you're old

STUART. Um

JOANIE. I mean older than me

STUART. Right it's been

JOANIE. Nine years Andy is five years older than me

STUART. Right

JOANIE. Do you have a job do you live in town

STUART. No I'm. visiting

JOANIE. Where do you live

STUART. Nebraska

JOANIE. *what*

STUART. What

JOANIE. Why do you live in Nebraska

STUART. ...uhhh

JOANIE. Because you're from *Springfield* why would you
move from *Springfield* Massachusetts to Nebraska

STUART. Why does anyone move anywhere

JOANIE. Do you have a job what do you do

STUART. I work at a bar

JOANIE. You moved to Nebraska to work at a bar

STUART. Well I moved to Nebraska with my girlfriend
because she was working on a farm there and then I
got a job in a bar and then we broke up and I still live
there

(**JOANIE** *nods knowingly.*)

JOANIE. I had a boyfriend we broke up

STUART. Is this the boyfriend at the methadone clinic

JOANIE. No that was a different boyfriend this one wasn't very smart I met him at HCC or I shouldn't say he's not smart I mean you could say he's smart about some things like trout fishing and motorcycles and Marxism and where to get weed from people

STUART. Uhhuh

JOANIE. But after a while it became clear he couldn't keep up with me so I ended it he still sends me lengthy text messages sometimes but mostly I ignore them

> (*Something happens in the previews which they look at.*)

What happened with your girlfriend

STUART. What happened?

JOANIE. Yeah like when did you break up

STUART. Um. Six months ago

JOANIE. *Why* did you break up

STUART. Um. I don't know it was just over there wasn't really like *A Reason*

JOANIE. There's *always a reason* like for me? you could say that I always break up with my boyfriends because they're not as smart as me and they can't keep up

STUART. Uhhuh

JOANIE. OR you could even say I actually *select* these particular individuals as a way to subconsciously self-perpetuate my abandonment issues initiated by the death of my dad

STUART. Woah ok

JOANIE. But you could also say that I break up with them because no one can ever truly replace my brother as my favorite person and so I give up on them before giving them any kind of chance at all

STUART. Right

JOANIE. So there's a reason there's *always a reason* you can tell me Stuart but also only if you want to and no pressure

(They watch the preview for a moment.
JOANIE *eats popcorn. After a moment:)*

STUART. Well I guess, um. that we grew apart? over time, that we wanted. Different things?

JOANIE. Uhhuh like what

STUART. Um like she's vegan?

JOANIE. Ugh

STUART. She works on like a farm and also at a small animal sanctuary

JOANIE. Like the animal sanctuary is small or it's for small animals

STUART. What?

JOANIE. You said it's a small animal sanctuary

STUART. Oh it's small but the animals are big or they're normal sized

JOANIE. Ok

STUART. And I just um. Eat whatever so that was you know. A Conflict.

JOANIE. Ok

STUART. And she wanted. Kids and wanted them to be vegan and I wasn't. Sure.

JOANIE. Ok

STUART. And she wanted. To live in Nebraska forever and I'm not. Sure.

JOANIE. Ok and what do you want

(Something happens on the screen and
STUART *looks at it. She watches him.)*

STUART. You ask a lot of questions.

*(***JOANIE*** looks right at him.)*

JOANIE. Oh. Do you want me to leave?

STUART. No it's ok

JOANIE. Because I can go back to my seat or also just leave

STUART. No that's not what I –. / You can

(**JOANIE** *starts to get up; it takes her a while to gather all her shit.*)

JOANIE. I can go I'll just go to my seat here keep the Mike and Ikes I don't know why I got them I don't / like them

STUART. No you don't have to

JOANIE. My mom tells me I have a problem with being intrusive so you just have to tell me if I'm being intrusive I get the / picture

STUART. No you're really not

JOANIE. Nice to meet you Stuart bye

(*She starts to walk away.*)

STUART. I want to learn how to grow. Herbs?

(**JOANIE** *looks at him.*)

I think that would be nice and then I can use them for cooking. I also want to learn how to cook.

JOANIE. Uhhuh

STUART. Also how to gamble? and make money in casinos I've been thinking about that for a long time, I think I'd be good at it

JOANIE. Huh ok

STUART. And I want to live in a very cold place? like Alaska or Greenland where there aren't people around for miles and miles and I need to put snow tires or chains on my car and where the power goes out for weeks at a time and I need to burn wood in my wood burning stove and sit in my bed with nine wool blankets and drink hot black coffee

JOANIE. Uh that sounds

STUART. I want to read books from the minute I wake up in the morning till the minute I fall asleep and never get tired and never need to get up and eat or go to the bathroom or talk to anyone. I want to start chewing tobacco so I can spit it out in a cup and talk slowly. I want to eat cheese and only cheese every day forever. I want to kill something and then make it come back to life. I want to

> (**JOANIE** *goes to* **STUART** *and gives him an improbably gigantic hug. Popcorn goes everywhere. She pulls back and they look at each other. After a moment.*)

The popcorn

JOANIE. Yeah

STUART. I was saving it for during the movie

JOANIE. Well I have a lot of other food

> (*Something happens in the preview. They look at the screen.*)

STUART. I'm gay.

JOANIE. Duh.

STUART. ...What do you mean *duh*

JOANIE. I mean I knew that because of the way you talked about your girlfriend and how you said you wanted *different things* and how you fixated on her vegan-ness and how she works at a small animal / sanctuary

STUART. I wasn't fixating those things were *really big issues* / for us

JOANIE. I'm sure they were I could just tell that you were talking about those issues but also you were talking about. Something else.

> (*She sits back down. They watch the preview. After a bit:*)

STUART. I'm not having Thanksgiving with my parents.

JOANIE. Really

STUART. Yeah I just. (Can't) this year.

JOANIE. Oh

> (*They watch the preview.*)

Why did you come back to Springfield then

STUART. I didn't know what else to do.

JOANIE. Right.

>   *(They watch the preview.)*

Do you want to watch movies with me all day?

>   (**STUART** *looks at her.*)

If you're worried about the meth heads who work here they don't care and they won't notice anyway you won't get in trouble

STUART. Yeah ok

JOANIE. I have more burgers if you want one. also here drink some soda

STUART. um

>   *(She just hands the soda to him. The lights dim further and the opening song* for the movie comes on. They watch.* **STUART** *takes a sip of her Huge Soda.)*

JOANIE. *(Whispering, because now the movie's starting.)* This movie sucks

STUART. What?

JOANIE. I saw it two weeks ago I told you that before

STUART. Why did you come back

JOANIE. It's the only one playing at 11:45

>   *(They watch the movie. After a moment,* **JOANIE** *reaches over and takes* **STUART**'s *hand.)*

Is that –

STUART. Yeah that's good that's ok.

>   *(They watch the movie.)*

the end

---

*A license to produce *this movie* does not include a performance license for any third-party or copyrighted music. Licensees should create an original composition or use music in the public domain. For further information, please see Music Use Note on page 3.

What Happened at
the Dolphin Show

Miranda Rose Hall

WHAT HAPPENED AT THE DOLPHIN SHOW was produced as part of the Samuel French Off Off Broadway Short Play Festival at the Classic Stage Company in New York City on August 11, 2017. The production was directed by Katie Lindsay and the music was composed by Michael Costagliola. The cast was as follows:

HEIDI . . . . Cleo Gray
LINDA . . . . Cristina Pitter
CHERYL . . . . Cat Crowley
CHORUS . . . . Rachael Balcanoff, Gwendolyn Boniface,
Elliot Frances Flynn, Elz Cuya Jones,
Sable Worthy, Victoria Libertore

CHARACTERS

HEIDI – ten-year-old girl

LINDA – her mother, a forty-year-old woman

CHERYL THE ANNOUNCER – a butch lesbian; ageless

WOMEN AT THE DOLPHIN SHOW – a chorus of seven to ten women who
represent a diversity of age, body type, race, and gender presentations

SETTING

Baltimore

TIME

Now

Scene One

(**HEIDI** *attempts to look at the audience.*)

(*She attempts to look at the women in the audience with a "normal attitude."*)

(*However, she discovers that when she looks at the women in the audience, she feels a tingle in her panty region.*)

HEIDI. Uhm –
oh no.

    (*She looks away.*)

    (*She attempts to look again.*)

    (*She tingles.*)

Uhm –
oh NO.

    (*She looks away.*)

    (*She attempts to look again.*)

    (*She tingles.*)

Uhm –
I –
AH!

    (**HEIDI** *runs away.*)

Scene Two

*(**HEIDI** hides.)*

LINDA. Heidi!

Heidi!

HEIDI!

*(**LINDA** enters.)*

What is going on, Heidi.

HEIDI. –

LINDA. What is going on! You're supposed to have your shoes on! We're late, Heidi! Hop to!

HEIDI. I'm not going.

LINDA. We cannot be late to meet your father. You know how he gets about the parking!

HEIDI. I'm not GOING!

LINDA. Hop to, Heidi –

HEIDI. I'M NOT GOING TO THE DOLPHIN SHOW!

LINDA. –

HEIDI. –

LINDA. –

HEIDI. –

LINDA. Woah.

Okay.

Volume.

Attitude.

HEIDI. I'm sorry.

I –

cannot

go

to the

dolphin show.

LINDA. Why not.

HEIDI. Because I can't!

LINDA. That's not a –

HEIDI. I can't, okay?! I can't I can't I can't!!

LINDA. Heidi.

Okay.

Listen to me.

You've got to clean up this attitude.

Because I cannot tell what's going on here,

and it is causing me distress.

But I do know

that your father

your LOVING FATHER,

has had to work every night for the past two weeks

because we want you to BE ABLE TO AFFORD TO
GO TO COLLEGE.

And your father,

your loving father,

has one night off – ONE NIGHT OFF – for the next
two weeks,

and you know what he decided to do?

With his ONE NIGHT OFF?

Let's stay home, I suggested.

Have taco night.

Order pizza.

Because I myself am exhausted

from working two jobs

and parenting.

But no, he said.

No.

No.

Heidi's been asking

about the Dolphin Show.

The ACCLAIMED Friday Night Dolphin Show

at the National Aquarium

right here in Baltimore.

HEIDI. Mom –

LINDA. So he said
let's go to the Dolphin Show.
AS A FAMILY.

HEIDI. Mom!

LINDA. So that
AS A FAMILY
we can spend QUALITY TIME TOGETHER
and create VERY SPECIAL MEMORIES
of YOUR PRECIOUS, CHERISHED CHILDHOOD.

HEIDI. Mom! I'm sorry! I'm sorry!

LINDA. Then put on your shoes. And get out the door.

HEIDI. No, I can't!

LINDA. There is nothing more disrespectful than being late,
Heidi! Think of the assumptions of disaster!

HEIDI. Mom –

LINDA. HEIDI PUT YOUR SHOES ON!

HEIDI. MOM I CAN'T GO!

LINDA. WHY NOT!

HEIDI. BECAUSE I'M AFRAID I'M GOING TO SPEND
THE ENTIRE TIME STARING AT THE WOMEN.

    (A long silence.)

I just can't stop – thinking about the women.

LINDA. At the dolphin show.

HEIDI. Yes.

LINDA. In the wetsuits.

HEIDI. Yes. And
in the audience.
Especially the audience.
Women in the audience with –

    *(**HEIDI** gestures.)*

LINDA. Breasts.

HEIDI. Yes.

And the –

LINDA. Hips.

HEIDI. Yes.

And the –

LINDA. Hair?

HEIDI. YES.

LINDA. Well –

HEIDI. Mom! My mind is going crazy.

My BODY is going crazy.

I'M GOING CRAZY

just thinking about ALL THOSE WOMEN at the dolphin show.

I can't stop – I just can't stop – THINKING about them and I've got this FUNNY FEELING in my –

and I have been TRYING and TRYING to get it to go away,

I have been PRACTICING trying to LOOK AT PEOPLE without this –

FUNNY FEELING

BUT IT WON'T GO AWAY

IT CAN'T GO AWAY

and THAT IS WHY I CANNOT GO TO THE DOLPHIN SHOW.

LINDA. I see.

Is this a funny feeling in your –

      (**LINDA** *indicates "panty region."*)

"Panty region."

HEIDI. Don't say that.

LINDA. Okay.

Well, to be honest with you honey,

you know you're growing up

when you feel a funny feeling in your

"panty region."

HEIDI. MOM –

LINDA. I'm serious Heidi!

And that has everything to do with – it's called, uh –
that is just a NORMAL aspect of being a human being.

And these – women –

HEIDI. PLEASE DO NOT SAY WOMEN.

LINDA. Heidi, you said it first, I'm just trying to –

HEIDI. Can we please just –

LINDA. Heidi, do you think that maybe you're –

HEIDI. I'M NOT! I'M NOT! I'M NOT! I'M NOT! I'M NOT!
I'M NOT! DON'T SAY THAT.

LINDA. –

HEIDI. Volume.

I'm sorry.

LINDA. Okay.

Okay.

Well,

I'm going to go out on a limb here and say that you are
feeling

a little out of sorts.

But, uh – whatever you are

is okay.

It's – okay.

But, uh –

I think you'll feel better if you get up and walk around.

I always feel better

when I get up and walk around.

And we are running late for your father.

So Heidi.

Listen to me.

If we stay here, we're going to have to keep – talking
about it.

If we go to the aquarium, I can promise that we won't
have to talk about it.

Ever again.

HEIDI. Do you promise.

LINDA. I promise.

HEIDI. On your life.

LINDA. It's 4:45.

(They leave.)

Scene Three

(The National Aquarium.)

(The Dolphin Show.)

(**CHERYL THE ANNOUNCER** *appears.*)

CHERYL THE ANNOUNCER. Hello ladies and...EVERYONE!
Welcome to the FRIDAY NIGHT DOLPHIN SHOW here at the NATIONAL AQUARIUM IN BALTIMOOOORE!
My name is CHERYL,
and
and I am looking for a SPECIAL GUEST
to HANG OUT WITH ME
RIGHT HERE
in front of the audience.
Wow!
Who is this coming into the Dolphin Show!

(It's **HEIDI.***)*

(**HEIDI** *freezes.*)

What is your name?

HEIDI. Uhm.
Heidi.

CHERYL THE ANNOUNCER. Heidi!
And what have you come here to see?

HEIDI. The uh
dolphins.

CHERYL THE ANNOUNCER. Is that right.
Well Heidi,
I'd like you to be my SPECIAL GUEST!
Just stand up here and
LOOK OUT AT THE AUDIENCE.

HEIDI. Oh no.

CHERYL THE ANNOUNCER. You'll love it.

Alright, everybody!

LET THE DOLPHIN SHOW BEGIN!

[MUSIC "EVERYBODY'S GAY"]

(The **WOMEN AT THE AQUARIUM** *dance and sing their way onstage.)*

(These are not highly-sexualized dancing women.)

(These are women at an aquarium.)

(**HEIDI** *starts to freak out.)*

WOMEN AT THE AQUARIUM.

OH! OW! OH! OW! OH! OW! HEIDI!
AND EVERYONE ELSE!
OH! OW! OH! OW! OH! OW! HEIDI!
AND EVERYONE ELSE!
OH! OW! OH! OW! OH! OW!
HEIDI!

WE'RE HERE FOR THE DOLPHINS
AND WE'RE HERE FOR THE SWIMMIN'
WE'RE HERE WHILE YOU FREAK OUT ABOUT
YOUR INTEREST IN WOMEN

BUT HEIDI, DON'T YOU FEAR THAT
FUNNY LITTLE FEELING
'CAUSE THAT'S THE SPARK THAT LIGHTS THE WORLD
NO MATTER WHO YOU'RE DEALING WITH
SEXUAL FRUSTRATION
SEXUAL FRUSTRATION
SEXUAL FRUSTRATION
SEXUAL FRUSTRATION

IT HAPPENS AT THE MOVIES
AND WHEN BUILDING A TERRARIUM
IT HAPPENS WITH YOUR PARENTS
AT THE NATIONAL AQUARIUM

SEXUAL FRUSTRATION
SEXUAL FRUSTRATION
SEXUAL FRUSTRATION

SEXUAL FRUSTRATION

LOOK: THERE'S LADIES WHO LIKE LADIES
AND GENDERQUEERS AND MEN
THERE'S ALL KINDS OF FOLKS TO LOOK AT
AND ALL KINDS OF ACUMEN!

BUT DON'T BE SCARED OF LOOKING
AT BREASTS AND HAIR AND HIPS
THERE'S SO MUCH YOU CAN LOVE ABOUT
THOSE LADY HANDS AND LIPS

'CAUSE
EVERYBODY'S GAY
EVERYBODY'S GAY
EVERYBODY'S GAY GAY GAY GAY GAY
AT LEAST A LITTLE BIT
EVERYBODY'S GAY
EVERYBODY'S GAY
EVERYBODY'S GAY GAY GAY
OR AT LEAST THEY MIGHT CONSIDER IT

IN TIME THIS FUNNY FEELING
WILL BE SOMETHING FUN TO FLAUNT
BUT FOR NOW RELAX, ENJOY THE SHOW,
AND LOOK AT WHO YOU WANT!

HEIDI. Oh my God these women!

WOMEN AT THE DOLPHIN SHOW. Sooo many women.

HEIDI. I want to look!
I've got to look!

WOMEN AT THE DOLPHIN SHOW. She wants to look!
She's got to look!

HEIDI. I'm looking at the WOMEN!
I LOVE TO LOOK AT WOMEN!
I'M LOOKING AT THE WOMEN!

WOMEN AT THE DOLPHIN SHOW. The women at the Dolphin
Show!
'CAUSE
EVERYBODY'S GAY
EVERYBODY'S GAY

EVERYBODY'S GAY GAY GAY GAY GAY
AT LEAST A LITTLE BIT

EVERYBODY'S GAY
EVERYBODY'S GAY
EVERYBODY'S GAY GAY GAY
OR AT LEAST THEY MIGHT CONSIDER IT

IN TIME THIS FUNNY FEELING
WILL BE SOMETHING FUN TO FLAUNT
BUT FOR NOW RELAX, ENJOY THE SHOW,
AND LOOK AT WHO YOU WANT!
LOOK AT WHO YOU WANT!

> *(Dolphins leap and dive.)*
>
> *(It is a Dolphin Show Extravaganza.)*

Scene Four

(**HEIDI** *looks at the audience.*)
(*She looks at women.*)

HEIDI. Hi, ladies.
Hello.
Hello.
Hello.
Hello.
It is so
so
nice
to see you.

(**HEIDI** *is happy forever.*)

End of Play